Perfect Destruction

AMY LAURENS

OTHER WORKS

Find other works by the author at www.amylaurens.com

Perfect Destruction

INKLET #81

AMY LAURENS

www.inkprintpress.com

Print ISBN: 978-1-922434-21-0
eBook ISBN: 9798201932756

www.inkprintpress.com

National Library of Australia Cataloguing-in-Publication Data
Laurens, Amy 1985 –
Perfect Destruction
40 p.
ISBN: 978-1-922434-21-0
Inkprint Press, Canberra, Australia
1. Fiction—Fantasy—Dark Fantasy 2. Fiction—Fantasy—Dragons & Mythical Creatures 3. Fiction—Short Stories

First Print Edition: May 2022
Cover image © Cocoparisienne via Pixabay
Cover design © Inkprint Press
Interior art © Amy Laurens

PERFECT DESTRUCTION

THE WIND HOWLS THROUGH THE towering forest as Kiana stomps her combat boots against the grassy ground to warm her feet. "Reckon they'll be much longer?" she says, adjusting her rifle in the crook of her arm.

Beside her, Heiman shrugs, carbon-fibre body armour blunting his movements. "Hope not. This wind's a killer."

Kiana casts a glance at the fence behind her: cast iron, eight feet high, practically indestructible. But clouds are gathering, pressure is building, and their shift ended ten minutes ago. "I'm going to climb the tree."

"Why d'you wanna do that for?"

A sharp crack. They both whirl around. A branch from a nearby elm lies on the ground, broken by the fierce wind.

"Place is giving me the creeps," Kiana says, neck prickling. It feels like ants are crawling over her waist and hips. She shifts, wriggles, but her body armour's doing its job well and she can't get the itches to quit.

Big, grey cumulo-nimbuses boil over the sun. The noise of the wind is fierce.

"Doesn't matter," she says. "Home tomorrow."

"Oh?" says Heiman. "Tour's over?" His voice is too light, too casual.

Kiana doesn't look at him. "I thought you knew. This is my last shift."

He shrugs, picking at his rifle's grip where the parts don't quite line up.

Rumbling sounds in the distance. Heli rotors, or just thunder? Kiana hops from one foot to the other. "Wish they'd bloody hurry up."

"I dunno," Heiman says, staring fixedly at the treetops. "I'm in no rush."

Kiana eyes him sideways. He knew today was her last day. Everyone knew. The shifts are posted on the public roster board; it's not like it was a secret.

The rumble dies away. Just thunder then. The storms roar like the devil here, but they're transient, gone in under an hour.

"I'm climbing the tree."

Heiman shrugs. "Suit yourself."

Kiana straps her rifle on her back, adjusts her boots, and heads over to the lookout tree, a giant lone redwood that stands sentinel above the forest.

She climbs the aluminium ladder to the platform that sways high above the fence and looks out.

To the north the trees—elms and oaks, ash and introduced silver birch—diminish and in the distance, bare hilltops poke through, grass long and yellow. To her left the sun should be slowly toiling towards the horizon, but the storm clouds bubble and bloom like ink in the otherwise-blue sky. No sign of helicopters in any direction and it's now—she checks—nearly twenty minutes past shift change. They've never been this late before.

She's going home tomorrow.

Cheek in her teeth, Kiana swings slowly southward. The iron fence stretches out below her, as far as she can see through the trees. It encloses a space hundreds of acres across, and she's never seen one of their charges in the flesh, but looking in there still gives her the creeps. Every tree is taller, straighter, shinier, everything lush and green and perfect. Blossoms on an old, abandoned orchard bear perfectly shaped petals, bloom into un-blemished fruits, drop picture-perfect seeds.

She blinks. Was that a flash of white amongst the trees? Adrenalin floods her body and her stomach feels like it's dropped back to earth.

She peers closely, but everything looks normal. With a forceful exhale, Kiana turns and crosses the platform to the ladder.

Another hum. Her head snaps around towards it, and there in the east like a giant black wasp: a helicopter powering towards her. Tension melts away and Kiana laughs.

"Heiman!" she shouts. "Heiman, they're here!" She waves to catch his attention, laughing and pointing at the helicopter. Home. They're here, and she's going home.

The humming rumble grows louder as Kiana climbs down the ladder. Midway down, she realises the noise has changed in tone. It's not just the helicopter anymore—but it doesn't sound like thunder, either.

"What is it?" Hayman calls to her.

She looks around, but the trees are blocking her view.

Hurriedly she scrambles to the top of the ladder again. Adrenalin floods through her: a unicorn, blinding white against the bright green grass, heading towards the fence. "Look out!" she screams. "Heiman, get away!"

He peers up at her, confusion knotting his brow, then turns slowly toward the enclosure.

The unicorn picks its way closer, like it has all the time in the world, and with every step the humming increases.

Kiana sees the moment Heiman spots the 'corn: his whole body stiffens, fingers tightening compulsively around his rifle.

"Shoot! Shoot it! Shoot it now!" she screams.

The unicorn covers another ten metres before Heiman collects himself enough to raise the herb-loaded rifle.

The unicorn stops and throws its head back, point arcing up towards the gathering storm.

Kiana runs her gaze across the sky and her heart skips another beat; the storm isn't coming, it's here.

And then in the same instant, three things happen: a shaft of crackling energy shoots up from the unicorn's point to the clouds; lightning strikes the redwood where Kiana clutches at the platform railing; Heiman remembers his rifle and pulls the trigger.

Kiana screams as the redwood's ancient trunk snaps, a deep sound like a canon firing, death and inevitable destruction.

She catches a quick glimpse of Heiman's face, staring up at her, mouth and eyes wide in horror.

She's grabbing blindly, wildly, for anything she can reach. As she clings to one of the platform's rails the tree falls, and she rides it all the way into the cast-iron fence.

The fence should stop her, catch the tree—but either the storm or the unicorn has done something to it and instead the impact of the tree snaps it like brittle candy.

It shatters on the ground, followed by the redwood—and Kiana.

Hurts.

She sucks air in, shallow gasps that don't help to restore the breath that's been knocked out of her. A voice fades in, like her ears had stopped working during the fall, or the crashing of the tree and fence and sky blocked everything out, or maybe even like the world had ended.

"Get away! Get away from her, you pissing beast!"

Kiana can't move her head yet; her entire view is sky, framed on one side by branches.

Heiman rushes into her field of vision, standing protectively over her while she gasps like a fish out of water. Hurriedly he empties the clip from his rifle and tries to load another—but his fingers are fumbling and he drops it in the grass.

White. The sky shouldn't be white.

Fur. The sky is neither white nor furry.

Kiana's eyes widen as she realises the unicorn is close enough to touch, if only she could remember how to make her arms and fingers work.

Before she can think too hard about why her arms and legs aren't working, why she should be in so much pain after a fall like that and instead can't feel a thing, before she can verbalise the niggling terror lurking in the depths of her mind that something is wrong, Wrong, WRONG, light explodes from the unicorn.

It's white and blinding in a way that no natural light could ever be: even the moon has warmth compared to this.

Her toes and fingers tingle. She can feel them. Her lungs burn, her hip—her hip is probably on fire.

Above her, Heiman groans, stumbles, falls to one knee.

"No," Kiana whispers as the burning in her lungs dies down. "No, you can't." But the unicorn's power is destroying him as fast as it's healing her, and when she leaps to her feet she's only just in time to catch him as he sways. He's too heavy for her to hold; she eases him slowly to the ground. "No," she tells him. "You passed medical. You passed!"

He smiles—tries to. It clearly hurts and his eyes unfocus through the pain.

"F... Faked genes," he breathes raggedly.

Kiana presses her eyes closed tightly against his confession. "You idiot."

"Never... mind," he gasps out, eyes pressed closed. "You're going... home tomorrow."

"Too right," Kiana says. "I'm not sitting by *your* bedside for a month while they genewash you."

He laughs, weakly. "Get out," he says and gestures to the sky with his eyes.

Kiana glances over her shoulder: the heli is landing. By the time she looks back, Heiman is gone. She grips him for a second longer, fingers knotting in the loose sleeves of his uniform. Then she gently lays him down and stands.

With deliberate, precise steps, she walks to the unicorn. She stares it in the eye, and languidly it stares back.

"You killed him. You *bastard*," she

spits, hands fisting at her sides. "You *killed* him."

The unicorn just stands there.

Kiana throws herself at the immovable beast. She hammers her fists against its neck, kicks its fetlocks and screams. Someone races in behind her, pins her arms against her sides. She screams again, wordless rage, clawing and biting at whoever holds her.

The air is dark green and savoury, herbal frabah rounds exploding, pop-pop-pop-pop-pop.

The unicorn shrieks. Kiana's head rings.

A white, glowing body rears—

Shrieks again, then stumbles to the ground.

The hands clamping Kiana's arms release her, and she falls. It hurts her knees. She doesn't care. She presses her hands over her face and cries.

The unicorn is dead—but so is Heiman.

THE MAKING OF *PERFECT DESTRUCTION*

Oh, the puricorns! One day, I will write a novel about these destructive unicorns. I even have a cover for it already, so I'd really better write the book.

For now, you get teasers like *Perfect Destruction*, and also *Purity*, Inklet #58.

These ultra-destructive unicorns came about one day as I speculated on unicorn mythology. We know that there is a historical connection between virgins and unicorns, or, more bluntly, between so-called purity and unicorns.

So what if that 'purity' applied to more than just someone's sexual activity? That's problematic enough right there; how much *more* problematic would it be to see that label of 'pure' applied everywhere else?

So we have the puricorns: unicorns that destroy synthetic materials, highly refined foods, human-created building materials, highly refined everything else, medicines... and who enforce the strictest standards of ableism. Because anyone with aberrant genes couldn't possibly be considered pure... *insert heavy sarcasm here*

(Interestingly, under this paradigm, it's ableism that's enforced, not racism, because there is no credible genetic basis for the social construct we call race.)

The mythology and magic* systems of this world are yet to be fully refined (no pun intended), but it *is* established that the unicorns are not fully sentient. They're not aware of the destruction they wreak.

Of course, that doesn't diminish the severity of the consequences, as we see in this story here.

* I say magic system, but really this is a science fiction world, with science fiction unicorns, whose horns propagate a kind of nano-reconstructive technology.

Read more by Amy Laurens!

RUSH JOB

ON THE POLISHED-WHITE PERSPEX DESK BY THE holovid, the tiny grey printer chattered. The little stream of paper it was sending out into the dim room was no more than a handsbreadth across, and in the blue light of the sleeping screens the paper glowed cerulean.

Jamie Evans leaned back in her moulded desk chair, waiting for the printer to finish. The warm scent of the ink clouded around her and she drummed her fingers on the desk, impatient to see what the orders would bring.

The printer chattered on.

Jamie glanced up at the holoscreens that towered from her desk surface right up to the roof, wrapping around her in a glowing blue semi-circle in the small, dark control room of her shuttle. The screens continued their sleep though, devoid of any new information.

Out of habit, she checked the nav-system: all clear, everything still on track, the shuttle scheduled to arrive at the space station Aphelion in a little over two hours.

Jamie drummed her fingers again as the printer continued its chatter.

Damn thing never was fast enough.

She stretched languidly in her chair, briefly considered that she should maybe grab something to eat as her stomach rumbled, then decided not as memories of her last visit to Aphelion surfaced.

Aphelion's marketplace was famous throughout the entirety of clean space, with every kind of food—and every kind of human—in attendance. Along with a fair few other things, including everything you usually had to travel to Clan Space for.

Jamie's lips quirked. Last time, she'd come away with a lifelong love for pecan cheesecake, a pocket scanner that should have taken two months and four thousand bucks to source if she'd done it legal, and a voucher for a dinner at Maxador, rumoured to be the best restaurant in not just this quadrant, but the entire galaxy.

Even the Witch Clans, it was rumoured, couldn't do better than Maxador.

Jamie stretched again and sighed. It was fifty-fifty whether she'd have time to cash in on that dinner on this trip. It all hinged on that strip of paper now trailing over the edge of the desk from the little printer.

The printer beeped, green light flashing.

Ha. At last. You'd have thought, Jamie mused, that in this day and age someone could invent a cryptron printer that was faster.

Jamie leaned forward, tore off the strip of paper, and turned it over. Arcane-looking symbols covered it in neat, diagonal lines. She squinted. She'd been receiving her orders in cryptron for eight years now, and despite the fact that it was designed to be an infallibly uncrackable cipher unless you had one of the patented and heavily legislated readers, some days she felt she was getting the hang of it. That series of markings there, for example.

Her heart sped up.

Unless she was highly mistaken, that little cluster meant a job with a tight deadline.

Jamie spun the chair around, tapped the control panel on the other side of desk to wake the reader, and fed the long slip of paper into the slot in the interface.

A portion of the screen at the lower

left lit up, white code streaming past on a blue background, designed not to provide any actually information, but merely to make it look like the machine was doing something useful. Jamie knew. She'd copied all the code down in her first year and broken it. *Lorem ipsum dolor sit amet...* It was all nonsense.

She drummed her fingers again.

The scent of warm spices curled around her.

"Hello-Alex?"

"Hello, Jamie," the ship's AI responded in soothing, neutral tones.

"Why can I smell yellow curry?"

"It is thirteen hundred ship time. It is time for you to ingest sustenance."

Jamie sighed. Forgetting to reschedule the automatic meal system wasn't the worst thing in the world. And if this really was a rush job the cryptron reader was presently decoding, maybe it was better to eat here first.

The lower-left screen flashed green. The torrent of nonsense code gave way to a series of runic markings on screen —Cyrillic, a millennia-dead language revived explicitly for this purpose when cryptron was invented, because there was no point having an unhackable cipher if you also had a machine that could simply translate it into Standard. There were legislations around ownership of the readers, sure, but it would be stupid to assume that in the whole history and use of cryptron, no one would ever illegally procure a reader. Or crack the code.

Cyrillic, though, Jamie could read no problem. The gist of the situation was this: in about nine hours, a deal was going down somewhere in the marketplace on Aphelion, probably Sector Q. Maybe P.

A rare—and priceless—stolen item was being traded.

The government needed the item

back. Jamie was to retrieve it.

There were more details, of course: general description of the item, possible parties involved in the trade, blah blah, etc etc.

Jamie stopped. Squinted at the page. Reread it, just to make sure her Cyrillic wasn't off.

The item she was supposed to collect was a spherical, gelatinous object about two feet in diameter. It was listed as organic, virtually indestructible, and preferring vacuum for long-term transport.

Jamie squinted again. "Hello-Alex?"

"Hello, Jamie."

"Read this." She motioned at one of Alex's many camera eyes set around the room, their lenses no more than an inch across. "What does this sound like to you?"

"Item category best fits that of a space egg."

Jamie's stomach flipped. "Yeah. That's what I thought."

There were still a few surviving species that did space eggs of that size, shape and colour. It was plausible—and probable—that this was no particularly big deal, just a species the IGP wanted their hands on. This was not the 2600s. Surrofish had died out over 400 years ago.

It was not a surrofish egg, because that would be stupid—and disastrous.

Jamie chewed at the inside of her lip.

A century or two after humans colonised space, they'd realised they weren't alone. There were other creatures out there in the black, not sentient, but smart in their own ways. These creatures lived in the vacuum, a complex, delicate ecosystem built on living particles similar to tardigrades—single-celled and nearly indestructible.

They formed the bottom of a food

web as complex and varied as the one built on plankton. And for the most part, these creatures of vacuum were about as dangerous to humans as ocean creatures were—keep out of their way and they'd keep out of yours.

Then the Witches, a group of super-powered and highly xenophobic humans, had found the surrofish, whose eggs could support the bacteria the Witches used to maintain their super-powers—and which sent normal humans fatally insane.

A surrofish egg could survive vacuum indefinitely, and at only two-feet in width, they were nigh undetectable to radars attuned to larger threats.

And loaded up with Witch bacteria, they could seed the terraforming of an entire planet, letting loose a pathogen that would destroy any clean humans on the planet within months.

It was the galactic equivalent to all-out nuclear warfare, and it only ended when the IGP—Inter-Galactic Police, the enforcement arm of the united government of clean-human space— had engineered a gene drive that sent the surrofish extinct.

A tiny, possibly concerned beep. "Is anything wrong?" Alex enquired.

Jamie shook her head, hauling herself out of the dark well of her thoughts. "No. I'm being absurd. Alarmist. Like the plague, you know? Mention a rat infestation and people's minds *still* go back to the great Earth plagues of the 1400s."

"I am aware of this connection."

Jamie sighed. So she had to retrieve a space egg. There were plenty of species that laid space eggs. Totally no big deal.

And if she worked fast enough, her IGP orders wouldn't interfere with her plans to see Nathaniel.

Again.

She rechecked the navsys. One hour

and forty-six minutes to prep. Plenty of time.

Right after she ate that curry.

Keep reading! Head to www.inkprintpress.com/amylaurens/witchblue/rushjob/ to buy your copy now!

ABOUT THE AUTHOR

AMY LAURENS is an Australian author of fantasy fiction for all ages. Despite writing about ultra-destructive varieties of equine, she actually really loves horses.

Amy has also written the award-winning portal-fantasy *Sanctuary* series about Edge, a 13-year-old girl forced to move to a small country town because of witness protection (the first book is *Where Shadows Rise*), the humorous fantasy *Kaditeos* series, following newly graduated Evil Overlord Mercury as she attempts to acquire a castle, the young adult series *Storm Foxes*, about love and magic and family in small town Australia, and a whole host of non-fiction and shorter works.

INKLETS

Collect them all! Released on the 1st and 15th of each month.

Shadows NEVER LIE
AMY LAURENS

Here She Lies
LIANA BROOKS

Perfect Destruction
An Age Of Unicorns Story
AMY LAURENS

What Blood Can Do
AMY LAURENS

Dancer, Dreamer Seer
LIANA BROOKS

As Time Whirls Slowly Past
AMY LAURENS

Far More Satisfying Than Hell
AMY LAURENS

Just Another Day In Hell
LIANA BROOKS

Moon AND Morning
AMY LAURENS

Some
Impropriety
Expected
AMY LAURENS

NEON SNOW
LIANA BROOKS

Reincarnation
LIANA BROOKS

More Than
Mushrooms
AMY LAURENS

DOUBLE ISSUE
How To Make A Star
& The World Ended
LIANA BROOKS

CAUGHT
IN THE ACT
AMY LAURENS

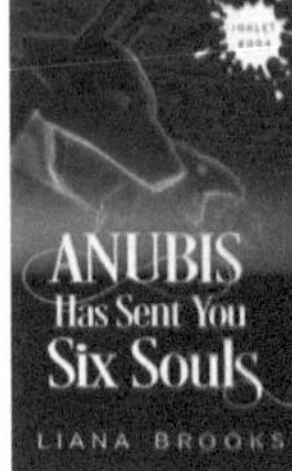

ANUBIS
Has Sent You
Six Souls
LIANA BROOKS

PRAYER TO A
GODDESS
LIANA BROOKS

Love In The
Time Of Corona
AMY LAURENS

9 781922 434210